THIS WALKER BOOK BELONGS TO:

First published 1987 by Walker Books Ltd
87 Vauxhall Walk, London SE11 5HJ

This edition published 1991

Text © 1987 Pam Ayres
Illustrations © 1987 Julie Lacome

Printed and bound in Hong Kong by
Dai Nippon (Pte.) Ltd

British Library Cataloguing in Publication Data
Ayres, Pam
Guess who?
I. Title   II. Lacome, Julie
823'.914 [J]
ISBN 0-7445-2034-7

Guess Who?

Written by
Pam Ayres

Illustrated by
Julie Lacome

WALKER BOOKS
LONDON

Piglets jumping off a bale, Who has lost his curly tail?

Mum and Richard
tap their feet,
Who is marching
down the street?

Penguins jump and
splash and play,
Which one caught
a fish today?

A birthday party!
James is three!
One boy's greedy.
Who is he?

Who has big strong teeth that gleam, And builds a dam to stop the stream?

Seven cows
all chew the cud,
Who likes rolling
in the mud?

The babies sit
on mummy's knee,
One is crying.
Who is she?

Two reindeer
are eating moss,
Which is happy?
Which is cross?

Someone's made
a shiny trail,
Can you find
a little snail?

Three fat pandas
up a tree,
One is sleeping.
Which is he?

Two boys running in the sports, Which of them has lost his shorts?

The moon is high,
the woods are deep,
Who is not
in bed asleep?

MORE WALKER PAPERBACKS
For You to Enjoy

SING A SONG OF SIXPENCE
illustrated by Julie Lacome

Fifteen favourite nursery songs, including Humpty Dumpty, Baa Baa Black Sheep,
Hush-a-bye Baby and Twinkle Twinkle Little Star.
"Satisfyingly firm and rich backgrounds of field or interior, and nice unusual details."
The Junior Bookshelf
ISBN 0-7445-1719-2   £3.99

GUESS WHAT?
by Pam Ayres
illustrated by Julie Lacome

The companion to *Guess Who?* – another delightful rhyming guessing
game by one of this country's most popular poets.
ISBN 0-7445-2035-5   £2.99

WHEN DAD CUTS DOWN THE CHESTNUT TREE
WHEN DAD FILLS IN THE GARDEN POND
by Pam Ayres
illustrated by Graham Percy

Two affectionate rhyming texts on a conservationist theme. The advantages and
disadvantages of a chestnut tree and a garden pond come under a child's scrutiny.
"Warm and engaging." *Susan Hill, Today*
ISBN 0-7445-1436-3   *When Dad Cuts Down the Chestnut Tree*
ISBN 0-7445-1437-1   *When Dad Fills in the Garden Pond*
£2.99 each

**Walker Paperbacks are available from most booksellers, or by post from
Walker Books Ltd, PO Box 11, Falmouth, Cornwall TR10 9EN.**

To order send: Title, author, ISBN number and price for each book ordered, your full name and address and a cheque or postal order
for the total amount, plus postage and packing: UK, BFPO and Eire – 50p for first book, plus 10p for each additional book to a
maximum charge of £2.00. Overseas Customers – £1.25 for first book, plus 25p per copy for each additional book.
Prices are correct at time of going to press, but are subject to change without notice.